SILK WOOD

ISBN 1 85854 146 8
Published by Brimax Books Ltd, Newmarket, England CB8 7AU 1995.
Printed in France.

SILK WOOD

BY

GILL DAVIES

ILLUSTRATED BY

ERIC KINCAID

Brimax · Newmarket · England

Fluffytuft has an Idea

————— · —————

"Nothing," said Mrs Squirrel, "can be sweeter than Silk Wood in Spring."

She was shaking her duster outside the front door of Little Tree House and had stopped for just a moment to look around at the morning.

White wood anenomes shone like stars in every sunlit glade and the banks were dappled yellow with primrose petals. Bluebells lapped around the tree trunks in a purple mist that stretched as far as the eye could see.

"Lovely, that's what it is!" said Mrs Squirrel to nobody in particular. "The birds are singing at the tops of their voices and the bluebells smell like heaven."

Mrs Squirrel sniffed the air happily, gave her duster another vigorous shake and then hurried indoors to chase away the cobwebs that hung like lace in every shaft of sunlight.

Young Fluffytuft Squirrel was pretending to be asleep. He pulled the quilt further up so that only the tip of his nose peeped out on the pillow. This was an unwise move as it revealed, at the other end of the bed, a row of very tiny, ticklish toes.

Mrs Squirrel had just picked up her feather duster to reach the highest cobweb when she spotted Fluffytuft's toes escaping from the covers. This was an opportunity not to be missed. In a flash, the feather duster whisked around to find the tiny toes and suddenly Fluffytuft was all of a squirm and a squeal and a squiggle and a giggle.

"Get off! Stop it! Don't! Leave me alone, I'm still asleep!" Fluffytuft protested, wrapping the patchwork quilt all around him and rolling into a ball in the middle of the bed.

Still the feather duster found a gap and danced on the end of Fluffytuft's pink nose. Fluffytuft sneezed and dropped the quilt.

"Go away! I'm asleep, I tell you!" he shouted, tumbling off the bed. "I am fast asleep. Surely you can see that I am fast asleep. Stop waking me up, will you."

Then he ran around his little bed and into the bathroom to put a stout wooden door between himself and the persistent feather duster.

"I assume you won't want any breakfast then," Mrs Squirrel called after him. "Young squirrels who are fast asleep find it extremely difficult to eat hot toast and peanut butter."

"I expect I'll manage," answered Fluffytuft, giving his face a brief wash before coming back out to put on red dungarees, a yellow shirt and his blue striped socks.

"What are you planning to do today?" asked Mrs Squirrel, staring crossly at a large spider that was creeping into the darkest corner of the hearth.

"I think," said Fluffytuft, between mouthfuls of toast oozing with peanut butter, "that I am going to lay an egg."

"Lay an egg!" exclaimed Mrs Squirrel, turning to look at Fluffytuft in amazement – but still keeping watch over the spider in case it dared try to spin any more cobwebs. "Don't be ridiculous, Fluffytuft. Squirrels don't lay eggs, only birds do that, and snakes and butterflies – and spiders." She made a rush with her feather duster at the spider on the hearth who scuttled quickly between the pile of logs and the copper kettle.

"Well, I don't care what ordinary squirrels do," went on Fluffytuft. "It is Spring. All the birds outside seem really pleased with the eggs they have in their nests; they have been singing about it all week. I should like to join in the fun and have an egg all of my own."

Fluffytuft carried his plate to the sink, popped it into the warm soapy water and then stepped out of the front door of Little Tree House into the warm sunshine.

Eric Kincaid

Silk Wood looked and smelled beautiful. It was a wonderful day – the perfect sort of day to lay an egg.

Fluffytuft scampered through the wood. Rosie Rabbit was waiting for him on Primrose Bank.

"Hi there, Fluffytuft!" said Rosie. "What are you doing this morning?"

"Today," announced Fluffytuft importantly, "I am going to lay an egg."

"Lay an egg!" laughed Rosie Rabbit. "You are silly, Fluffytuft. Squirrels don't lay eggs. What a funny idea!"

Fluffytuft was cross. "You are very rude to laugh at me, Rosie," he said. "If you are just going to sit there and snigger, I shall go on my own."

So Fluffytuft left Rosie Rabbit sitting on Primrose Bank, dabbing at her tears of laughter with a handkerchief, and he set off alone down the woodland path.

As Fluffytuft marched along towards the stream, the woodland creatures came out to watch. Fluffytuft was full of ideas that no-one understood but they liked to see him in his red dungarees, yellow shirt and smart blue striped socks. Fluffytuft was full of fun. He made them laugh. He was smiling now as he strode along.

"I am going," Fluffytuft said, "to find my egg. And I expect I shall have an adventure today – and Spring in Silk Wood is quite the nicest place to have one, don't you think?"

And the birds watched and chirruped and sang, proudly sitting on their nests, snug full of eggs, and wondered what Fluffytuft would get up to next. A squirrel lay an egg indeed!

But Fluffytuft's funny ideas were to be the start of a good many adventures in Silk Wood.

———— • ————

Fluffytuft
Lays an Egg

———— • ————

Fluffytuft Squirrel sat down by the waterfall and watched the bubbles dancing in the sunlight, tiny flashes of rainbow dancing inside them.

"I do like waterfalls," he said to the kingfisher who was darting across the stream. "They make such a lovely, gurgly-splurgly, dashing-splashing, rushing-gushing sound, don't you think?"

"Hmmm . . . " replied the kingfisher. "That's a lot of words for a little squirrel like you. Now do be quiet please and let a fellow concentrate. Fishing is a serious business you know." And the kingfisher went back to his branch, ever ready to dive for a lunch dressed in silver scales.

Just then Rosie Rabbit came skipping over the bridge and round to the edge of the grassy river bank to where Fluffytuft was resting.

"There you are, Fluffytuft," she called out happily. "I've been looking for you everywhere. Have you found an egg to hatch yet? Surely your tail is too fluffy to sit on a nest like a bird?"

Fluffytuft frowned. "Don't you dare laugh at me again," he said. "I shall find myself an egg very soon, so there, Rosie Rabbit. I don't see why a squirrel can't have an egg to hatch if he wants. Why should the birds have all the fun?"

Fluffytuft stood up, shook his tail angrily and set off along the bank at a merry pace before Rosie could catch him up again.

"What a cross little squirrel he is today," said Rosie Rabbit.

"Doesn't do to laugh at other peoples' ideas, you know," said the kingfisher. "Hurts a fellow's feelings. Now do be quiet please and let me fish."

Fluffytuft was running so quickly he didn't notice the sudden twist of tree roots across the top of the bank.

A moment later he was slipping and falling, tumbling and rolling, flying and then lying in the muddy shallows at the edge of the river.

"Goodness," he said, "I'm soaking wet and my bottom's all muddy." And then he saw it. There, cushioned in a soft hollow at the edge of the bank, half hidden by silvery grass, was a round, white object.

Fluffytuft stared. He rubbed his eyes and looked again. "It is," he said. "Yes, it is, it really is. It's an egg."

It lay there, cool and shiny, white and perfectly smooth. Fluffytuft looked around him cautiously. No-one seemed to be guarding the egg. Certainly no-one was sitting on it. This was an egg that was up for grabs!

"Hello, little egg," said Fluffytuft, tenderly scooping up the egg and cupping it in his paws. "I'm Fluffytuft Squirrel and from now on, you are MY egg. I shall look after you and make sure you hatch."

What Fluffytuft did not realise in his excitement was that this was not actually an egg at all. It was a pebble, a very beautiful pebble – smooth and shiny and speckled – but a pebble, none the less.

Fluffytuft carried his egg back up to the top of the slope. There he built a mound with the softest grass and moss he could find, made a dent in the middle and laid the egg carefully on top.

"There," he said, "I've laid an egg. Who said a squirrel couldn't do that? Now all I have to do is sit on my egg and wait for it to hatch."

He perched his bottom on top of the nest and thought how lucky he was to have found his egg at last. He sat there a long time but the egg did not seem ready to hatch just yet.

Fluffytuft sat there all afternoon and then began to wonder what he would do when the egg did hatch.

He was not quite sure how he would catch all the worms a baby bird might need. He didn't much like the idea of it. That is, of course, if this was a bird. What if it was a snake's egg!

This thought rather worried Fluffytuft and he jumped up hurriedly to take another look at his infant – but the egg was nowhere to be seen! Had it hatched already and run away without Fluffytuft noticing? At that moment Rosie Rabbit came round the corner.

"I'm sorry if I was rude, Fluffytuft," said Rosie, "I didn't mean to hurt your feelings . . . but, why, whatever is the matter?"

"Oh, Rosie," cried Fluffytuft, "I found my egg and tried to hatch it but now it has run away." He turned away to hide the big tear that was sliding down his cheek.

Rosie peered at the nest and then put her paw gently through the moss. There was something heavy at the bottom. Rosie lifted it out.

"This isn't an egg at all," said Rosie, trying not to giggle. "It's a pebble. It's so heavy it has fallen through to the bottom of your soft little nest. You are silly, Fluffytuft!"

Fluffytuft stared at the 'egg' and began to laugh. "I am," he said, "a silly, fried-banana, ninny-winny squirrel!" And he laughed so much he had to roll on the ground and hold his tummy and kick his legs in the air.

Then Fluffytuft carried the 'egg' back to Little Tree House. There, he and Rosie found his paint box and put bright stripes and flowers all over the pebble and gave it to Mrs Squirrel as a present.

"How lovely!" said Mrs Squirrel. "Do you know, if it wasn't for all the stripes and flowers, you could almost think this pebble was an egg – now what is the matter with you two? What's so funny?"

She smiled and put Fluffytuft's 'egg' on the shelf. And that night Fluffytuft dreamed he was hatching an egg as big as a ball and it was full of striped and flowery baby pebbles with bright orange beaks.

———— • ————

Eric Kincaid

Fluffytuft Discovers his Tail

———— • ————

Fluffytuft Squirrel had a wonderful tail. Ever since he had been born, folks had remarked upon it; it was fluffy, it was handsome, it was an adorable shade of red, wasn't he a lucky little squirrel?

Fluffytuft was delighted everyone liked his tail so much. He even let Mrs Squirrel brush out the tangles and knots without complaining too loudly.

The trouble was he could not actually see his tail. He would twist around and peer behind him but the tail bounced out of view. He quickly turned the other way but the tail always disappeared just out of sight.

Fluffytuft balanced on the chair to look in Mr Squirrel's shaving mirror but there wasn't room to turn around.

He stood on tiptoe on the bed but the mirror on the wall was too high. He had to bounce up and down to catch a glimpse of his handsome red tail flashing past.

So one fine Summer afternoon, Fluffytuft set off to the edge of Silk Wood, where the wood gave way to Buttercup Meadow. For there lay the Silver Pool where the deer came to drink.

On a sunny day this great sheet of water acted like an enormous mirror and many animals came to drink the clear, sparkling water and to peep shyly at their reflections. This might be the place, Fluffytuft thought, to take a proper look at his fluffy, red tail.

Fluffytuft bounced along through the woods, picking sweet strawberries to eat, until suddenly the trees thinned and there was the Silver Pool, glinting in the sunlight.

Beautiful, creamy lilies were scattered over the pool and dragonflies zoomed and dived like tiny helicopters over the gleaming water.

Eric Kincaid

There on a lily pad sat Glurk the Frog, a poet and musician who sang songs to the moon each night.

"Hello," said Glurk. He flicked his tongue in and out, smiling right from one side of his face to the other. Then he croaked:

"No frog can be perfect, for a frog can't be,
But so far as frogs go, I'm as perfect as can be!"

"Of course," said Fluffytuft. "Now can you tell me where I should go to get the best view of my tail?"

"Over Buttercup Meadow, beyond the willow tree,
Where the sun slants down and the Summer breeze is free."

Fluffytuft thanked him and set off around the Silver Pool to where the water shone like a perfect mirror. There he stood and looked and gazed and saw a wonderful, handsome, fluffy, adorable red tail.

"Oh my goodness! Is that tail really mine?" he asked.

"Certainly not," said a voice. "It's mine."

Smiling at him with twinkling eyes, was a cheeky looking fox cub.

"Excuse me," said Fluffytuft nervously. "But aren't fox cubs like you meant to eat little squirrels like me?"

"I can't say I care much for that idea," said the fox cub. "You look as if you'd be more fun as a friend than a dinner. Frisky Fox is the name – but that tail you are admiring is mine, make no mistake."

Fluffytuft looked at the fox cub's cheery face, peered into the water and then said, "I don't like to argue the minute we meet, Frisky, especially as you seem such a friendly chap, but, I assure you that it is not your tail. It's mine."

"You are both wrong," said Glurk who had hopped across to join them.

"That tail in the water belongs to both of you.
Standing close together you cannot see it's two.
Your tails are joined as one in that mirrored water scene.
Move apart, you silly pair, you'll see just what I mean."

So the little animals stepped apart and there in the water were TWO wonderful, handsome, fluffy, adorable red tails.

Frisky and Fluffytuft were very pleased to see what beautiful tails they both had and from that moment on became the greatest of friends.

Now Glurk was a fine artist as well as a poet, so he sat there in the warm afternoon and painted the squirrel and the fox cub playing and laughing together.

Eventually the afternoon cooled, dusk fell and the two new friends trotted off homewards, promising to meet again soon.

The next morning a present was delivered to them both from Glurk the Frog – a portrait of the two friends comparing their handsome red tails.

"I do not need a mirror any more," said Fluffytuft, as Mrs Squirrel hung the painting above the fireplace. "I can look at my tail all the time now. Aren't I lucky?"

———— • ————

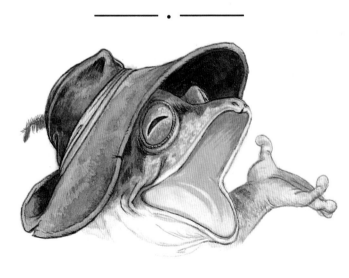

The Surprise Party

———— • ————

Fluffytuft woke up early and wondered why he felt so excited.
Then he remembered. Today was Old Man Otter's birthday and
there was to be a surprise party for him by the Silver Pool. Since
he slept so much he would know nothing about the party until
the evening – by which time all his friends would have arrived,
ready to celebrate.

"What are we going to give Old Man Otter for a present?" asked
Fluffytuft at breakfast.

"I've no idea," said Mr Squirrel, eating a bowl of nuts. "He has
everything an otter needs, so far as I can tell."

"Hmmm," said Mrs Squirrel, thinking as she sipped her
blackberry juice. "He's a dear old soul and deserves a special
present. I know, I shall bake him a birthday cake."

"And I," said Mr Squirrel, "will make him a new deckchair."

"What about me?" complained Fluffytuft, "I want to give him a
present too."

Eric Kincaid

"Then you," said Mr Squirrel, "will have to think of something yourself. Your mother and I are going to be very busy." He set off to his workshop and Fluffytuft scampered behind.

"I know," said Mr Squirrel, laughing, "why don't you lay him an egg?"

Mrs Squirrel came out to close the door which Fluffytuft always left open. "You could paint him a nice picture," she suggested.

"No," said Fluffytuft. "That's silly!"

"Why not make him one of your clever little calendars?" she said.

"No," said Fluffytuft. "That's boring!"

Mrs Squirrel tried again . . . "How about one of your newspaper hats?"

"No," said Fluffytuft. "That's a really stupid idea!"

"Oh, I don't know," said Mrs Squirrel, exasperated. "There's no need to be rude, Fluffytuft."

She went into the larder to fetch flour and currants.

"I was in a good mood when I woke up," said Fluffytuft, "but now I am feeling cross. I think I will go for a walk to calm down."

Fluffytuft met Rosie Rabbit by the waterfall. "What are you giving Old Man Otter as a birthday present?" he asked her.

"I don't know," said Rosie.

"Nor me," said Fluffytuft, brightening up. "I'm glad I am not the only one."

"Perhaps," said Rosie. "If we sit here and think really hard, we might have an idea."

The two friends sat and thought and thought until the morning was nearly gone and Frisky Fox came running along the path.

"Hi there," called Frisky. "I've been looking for you two everywhere. Glurk the Frog has written a song for us to sing at Old Man Otter's party. Come on, hurry along. We have to learn the words and the tune and practise until it is perfect. Glurk is going to play his violin."

They ran along to join Glurk who taught them his song. It was all about Old Man Otter and explained what a dear, kindly, smiling sort of fellow he was, how he knew every little animal for miles around and always had lots of stories and jokes to tell.

Glurk made them practise the song many, many times until they could sing it perfectly. Then they ran home to put on their best clothes and get ready for the party.

At last the evening arrived. From every corner of Silk Wood the animals came out into the shadows, carrying lanterns and tiptoeing through the moonlit wood.

A great feast had been set out, and the edge of Silver Pool was ringed with glowing lights.

Old Man Otter woke, yawned, stretched and went outside to see which stars were shining. What a surprise he had when he saw all his friends there, cheering and clapping, as swans came gliding over the water, carrying streamers and balloons.

Old Man Otter loved his new deckchair and the birthday cake, decorated with sugar fish.

But most of all Old Man Otter liked the song. The little friends sang out so sweetly under the stars that a few tears trickled into Old Man Otter's whiskers, especially when Fluffytuft, who had a very good voice sang the last two lines on his own:

"You're the dearest old otter in the world, you see,
We love you very much – Frisky, Rosie, Glurk and me."

Afterwards Old Man Otter shook their paws saying, "What clever fellows you are. Your song was quite the most beautiful present of all," and he hummed the tune quietly to himself for the rest of the evening.

Then they ate and danced and laughed and said it was the best party they had ever known.

At last they stumbled home, too sleepy as they slipped into bed to notice the pale pink and gold threads of dawn streaking the skies above Silk Wood.

Another day was beginning.